Kou-Skelowh / We Are The People

A Trilogy of Okanagan Legends

How Food Was Given
How Names Were Given &
How Turtle Set The Animals Free

Illustrated by Barbara Marchand

Theytus Books Ltd.
Penticton, B.C.

Library and Archives Canada Cataloguing in Publication

Kou-skelowh = We are the people : a trilogy of Okanagan legends / illustrated by Barbara Marchand. -- Rev. ed.

Complete contents: How food was given -- How names were given -- How turtle set the animals free.
ISBN 1-894778-18-9

1. Okanagan Indians--Legends. 2. Legends--British Columbia. 3. Animals--Folklore. I. Marchand, Barbara II. Title: We are the people.

E99.O35K68 2004 j398.2'089'97943
C2004-906483-5

We acknowledge the support through the En'owkin Okanagan Language program including translations by Andrew McGinnis, Delphine Derrickson, Richard Armstrong, Jeannette Armstrong, and Dr. Anthony Mattina.

We acknowledge the financial support of the Government of Canada through the Book Publishing Industry Development Program (BPIDP) for our publishing activities.

We acknowledge the support of the Canada Council for the Arts which last year invested $20.3 million in writing and publishing throughout Canada.

Nous remercions de son soutien le Conseil des Arts du Canada, qui a investi 20,3 millions de dollars l'an dernier dans les lettres et l'édition à travers le Canada.

We acknowledge the support of the Province of British Columbia through the British Columbia Arts Council.

CONTENTS

Editorial Note for Parents and Teachers

The original *Kou-skelowh Series* was published with black and white illustrations by Theytus Books in 1984, when the series won a Children's Book Centre "Children's Choice Award." In 1991 the *Series* was reformatted and published with new full colour illustrations by Barbara Marchand. In 1999, the three legends were reformatted and published under one cover. Now the legends have been translated into the Okanagan language in this new revised edition.

One of the most valuable aspects of the *Kou-skelowh Series* is how it was developed with Aboriginal cultural protocol. In 1981 the Okanagan Elders Council was approached and asked if some traditional legends could be used in the project. When the Elders gave permission for three legends to be used, they were translated into English. The English versions were then taken back to the Elders Council for examination and edited until they were approved for educational use by Okanagan children.

The Elders Council was then asked if Theytus Books could have permission to publish the legends for sale in the book trade. After lengthy discussions, Theytus was granted permission on the grounds that several conditions were met, including that no individual would claim ownership of the legends or benefit from the sales. The Elders Council also named the series "Kou-skelowh," meaning "we are the people." The series is "authorless" and copyrighted to the Okanagan Tribal Council.

The methodology that was used in the *Kou-skelowh Series* could stand as a model in which all possible concerns with Aboriginal cultural protocol were dealt with in a proper manner, as well as an example of the uniqueness of Aboriginal editorial practice.

Kou-Skelowh/We Are the People

An Okanagan Legend

HOW FOOD WAS GIVEN

ɬ‿t’ək’ʷək’ʷxíx iʔ‿tmix tə‿ksc’íɬnsəlx

In the world before this world, before there were people,

i‿l‿ cəxʔítms axáʔ iʔ‿təmxʷuláxʷ, i‿lútiʔ ła‿ksqilxʷ

and before things were like they are now, everyone was alive .

uł i‿lútiʔ iʔ‿stim’ t’a‿c’ x̌ił t‿ʕapnáʔ, yaʕt əcxʷəl’xʷált

and walking around like we do.

uł əc’aʔx̌əlwísəs c’x̌ił t‿mnímłtət.

All Creation talked about was the coming changes to their world.

yaʕt iʔ‿tmixʷ tqʷaʔqʷʔalmís iʔ ksck’ł̓ʔists iʔ‿təmxʷúlaʔxʷsəlx.

They had been told that soon a new kind of people

cúnmaʔlx cəm’ itlíʔ lut ksq’sápíʔs cəm’ əct’íxʷəlm iʔ‿sqilxʷ

would be living on this earth.

kst’alaʔxʷílxaʔx aláʔ i‿l‿təmxʷúlaʔxʷ.

Even they, the Animal and Plant people would be changed.

K’ʷam, yaʕtəlx, a‿ck’núsəs uł iʔ‿spəl’úlaʔxʷ cəm’ ksck’ł̓ísaʔx.

Now they had to decide how the People-To-Be would live

ʕapnáʔ kskc’x̌ʷíplaʔisəlx stim’ iʔ st’əlsqílxʷ i‿kłnxʷəlxʷəltáns

and what they would eat.

uł stim’ iʔ ksc’asʔístsəlx.

The four Chiefs of all Creation are:

iʔ‿kmúsməs iʔ ylyəlmíxʷms yaʕt iʔ‿tmixʷ ʔaxáʔəlx:

Black Bear, Chief for all creatures on the land

skəmxíst, ylmixʷm x̌əl yaʕt a‿c'aʔx̌əlwís i‿l‿tmxʷúlaʔxʷ

Spring Salmon, Chief for all creatures in the water

ntytyíx, ylmixʷm x̌əl yaʕt a‿ck'əwwílx k'a‿nyxʷtitkʷ

Bitterroot, Chief for things under the ground

sp'íƛəm, ylmixʷm x̌əl yaʕt k'a‿nixʷtúlaʔxʷ

Saskatoon Berry, Chief for things growing on land

síyaʔ, ylmixʷm x̌əl yaʕt iʔ‿spəl'úlaʔxʷ

They held many meetings and talked for a long time

taɬt xʷʔit sʔúl'uʔsəlx uɬ tqʷaʔqʷʔal'mísəlx talí q'sápiʔ

about what the People-To-Be would need to live.

stim' iʔ‿st'əlsqílxʷ i‿kɬnx̌əstáns mi cxʷəlxʷáltəlx.

All of the Chiefs thought and thought.

yaʕt iʔ‿ylyəlmíxʷm ənʔawqnwíxʷ.

"What can we give to the People-To-Be to eat that

"stim' caʔkʷ iʔ‿ksxʷíc'ɬtəm iʔ st'əlsqílxʷ ta‿ksc'íɬnsəlx

is already here on earth?" they asked one another.

a‿cwáy' aláʔ i‿l‿tmxʷúl'aʔxʷ?" sunwíxʷəlx.

"There seems to be no answer."

"wam' t'iʔ lut kʷu‿t'a‿kɬp'əlk'cín"

Finally, the three other Chiefs said to Bear, "You are the

xʷuy uɬ iʔ‿tkaʔkaʔɬís iʔ‿ylyəlmíxʷm cúsəlx skəmxíst "anwí

oldest and wisest among us.

iʔ‿kʷ‿misƛ̓əx̌ƛ̓x̌áp uɬ iʔ‿kʷ‿mispəx̌páx̌t tl‿mnímɬtət.

You tell us what you are going to do."

anwí mi kʷ‿cut kʷ‿səxkínaʔx,"

Bear said, "Since you have all placed your trust in me,

skəmxíst cut, "ałíʔ xʷəlk'ʷam, yaˁyáˁt kʷu‿tkʷílsmntəp,

I will have to do the best I can."

kn‿ksq'ʷəłmístaʔx məł talíʔ kn‿kswítmist."

He thought for a long time and finally he said,

ixíʔ sk'łpáx̌əms talí tə‿q'sápiʔ xʷu··y uł cut,

"I will give myself, and all the animals that I am Chief over, to be

"n'uʔs t'ək'ʷntín iscxʷəlxʷált, məł nixʷ yaˁt iʔ‿tmixʷ

food for the People-To-Be."

a‿ckyəlmxʷíplaʔstn, x̌əl ksc'iłns iʔ‿st'əlsqílxʷ"

Then he said to Salmon, "What will you do?"

xiʔ uł cus ntytyix, "stim' cəm' anwí aksck'ʷúl?"

Salmon answered, "You are indeed the wisest among us.

ntytyix cut, "anwí ta‿uníxʷ iʔ‿kʷ‿mispəx̌páx̌t

I will also give myself and all the things that live in the water

incá nixʷ ikst'k'ʷám iʔ‿scxʷəlxʷált naʔł yaˤt a‿ck'əwílx

for food for the People-To-Be."

x̌əl ksc'iłns iʔ‿st'əlsqílxʷ."

Bitterroot, who was Chief of all the roots under the

sp'íƛəm, iʔ‿ylmixʷm x̌əl yaʕt iʔ‿saʕx̌ʷíp i‿l‿sk'łixʷútms iʔ

ground said, "I will do the same."

‿tmxʷúlaʔxʷ, cut "incá nixʷ kn‿kst'iʔc'x̌íłaʔx"

Saskatoon Berry was last. She said, "I will do the same.

síyaʔ a‿c'iwt. síyaʔ cut, "incá nixʷ kn‿kst'ix̌íl'aʔx.

All the good things growing above the ground will be food for the

yaˁt iʔ‿x̌ast a‿cplal i‿l‿tmxʷúlaxʷ ksc'iłns

People-To-Be."

iʔ‿st'əlsqilxʷ"

Chief Bear was happy because there would be

iʔ‿ylmixʷm skəmxíst talíʔ npiyíls aɬíʔ way' cem'

enough food for the People-To-Be.

put‿iʔ‿ksc'iɬns iʔ‿st'əlsqílxʷ.

Bear said, "Now, I will lay my life down to make these things

skəmxíst cut, "ʕapnáʔ, ikst'ək'ʷám iscxʷəlxʷált ixíʔ mi kɬtr'ar'

happen."

iʔ kɬcáwtət."

Because the great Chief Bear had given

aɬíʔ tə‿ssílxʷaʔs t‿ylmixʷm skəmxíst t'ək'ʷntís

his life, all of Creation gathered and sang songs to bring

iʔ‿scxʷəlxʷálts, yaʕt iʔ‿tmixʷ ʔúl'uʔs uɬ nqʷníməlx kswítsəlx

him back to life.

kɬt'əlsqílxʷaʔx.

That was how they helped heal each other in that world.

ta‿ck'liʔ ki a‿ckənkənxtwíxʷəlx pnicíʔ i‿l‿tmxʷúlaʔxʷ.

They all took turns singing, but Bear did not

yaʕyáʕtəlx knanaqsmístəlx nqʷníməlx, náx̌əmɬ skəmxíst lut

come back to life.

t'a‿ɬt'əlsqílxʷ.

Finally, it came to Fly. He sang, "You laid your body down.

xʷu··y k ɬkicx k'əl x̌əx̌máˤɬ. nqʷnim uɬ cut, "t'ək'ʷntíxʷ asqíltk.

You laid your life down."

t'ək'ʷntíxʷ ascxʷəlxʷált."

His song was powerful. Bear came back to life.

iʔ‿qʷíləms talíʔ k'ʷəck'ʷáct. xiʔ skəmxíst st'əlsqílxʷs.

Then Fly told the four Chiefs, "When the People-To-Be

xiʔ x̌əx̌máˤɬ cus iʔ‿kmúsməs iʔ‿ylyəlmíxʷm, "iʔ‿st'əlsqílxʷ

are here and they take your body for food, they will sing

ɬcyaˤp uɬ ɬa‿ckʷístsəlx asqíltk x̌əl sc'iɬn, kscnqʷístsəlx

this song. They will cry their thanks with this song."

axáʔ iʔ‿qʷilm. cəm' sc'qʷaqʷ a‿nlímtnsəlx axáʔ t‿qʷilm."

Then Bear spoke for all the Chiefs, "From now on when the

xiʔ skəmxíst tqʷəlqʷəltíplaʔs yaˤt iʔ‿ylyəlmíxʷm, "tl‿ˤapnáʔ

People-To-Be come, everything will have its own song."

ɬə ciyáˤp iʔ st'əlsqílxʷ, yaˤt stim' cəm' i‿kɬqʷílm."

"The People-To-Be will use these songs

"iʔ‿st'əlsqílxʷ kə‿ck'ʷúləmstsəlx iʔ‿qʷilm

to help each other as you have helped me."

məɬ kənkənxtwíxʷəlx c'x̌iɬ ta‿mnímɬəmp iʔ‿kʷu‿knxítntəp."

That is how food was given to our people.

ta‿ck’liʔ ki iʔ‿sc’iɬn x̌ʷic’ɬtm iʔ‿cwílxtət.

That is how songs were given to our people.

ta‿ck’liʔ ki iʔ‿qʷilm xʷíc’ɬtm iʔ‿cwílxtət.

That is how giving and helping one another was and still

ta‿ck’liʔ ki i‿sxʷic’x uɬ i‿skənkənxtwíxʷ tl‿pnicíʔ uɬ way’

is taught to our people.

ʕapnáʔ ka cmaʔmáyaʔ k’əl‿iʔ‿cwílxtət.

That is why we must respect even the smallest, weakest persons
səc'x̌ílx kə chaʔstím iwá łə sw'íw'aʔt kəm' łə x̌ʷupt iʔ‿sqilxʷ
for what they can contribute.
x̌əl i‿ksckənxíts.

That is why we give thanks and honour to what is given to us.
səc'x̌ílx ki kʷu‿kəclímtaʔx uł kə cx̌aʔx̌aʔstím iʔ‿sxʷíc'əc'xtət.

Kou-Skelowh/We Are the People

An Okanagan Legend

HOW NAMES WERE GIVEN

iʔ‿skʷist ł‿xʷíc'łtməlx

A long time ago there were only Animal People on this earth.

q’sápiʔ t’i kmix iʔ‿tmixʷ iʔ‿ac’ax̌əlwísəs aláʔ i‿l‿təmxʷúlaxʷ.

There were no human beings like you and me.

lut t’a ksqílxʷ c’x̌ił t‿anwí kəm’ t‿incá.

It was a time when animals were like people.

pnicíʔ yaʕyáʕt iʔ‿tmixʷ c’x̌ił tə‿sqilxʷ.

They could laugh and talk and play and lived just

əcʕayʕayncútəlx uł əcqʷaʔqʷʔáləlx uł əc’ícəckn uł əcxʷəlxʷát

like you and I do.

c’x̌ił t‿anwí uł incá.

One day, the Great Spirit called all the Animal People

naqs sx̌əlx̌ʕált, iʔ‿k’ʷəl’ncútn x̌əlíts yaʕt iʔ‿tmixʷ

together.

ksʔúl’uʔsaʔxəlx.

They were told that there would be a great change on the earth,

cúntməlx cəm’ iʔ‿tmxʷúlaʔxʷ talíʔ kst’íxʷəxʷlaʔx,

and there would be new People coming to live with

uł i‿st’əlsqílxʷ kst’alaʔxwílxaʔx ksk’ʷúlaxəlx tə‿nək’ʷłcwíltn

the Animal People.

naʔł iʔ‿tmixʷ.

However, before they came, all of the Animal People would have

náx̌amł, i‿lútiʔ łə‿kscyáʕpsəlx, məł yaʕyáʕt iʔ‿tmixʷ cəm’

to change.

ksck’łʔí·saʔx.

They would be given names and, with each name,

yaʕyáʕt cəm’ tawłskʷíst uł əctəkxán i‿l‿stawskʷístəlx,

they would have a special job to do.

iʔ‿ksck’łtar’səlx.

They were told to gather the next day for their name-giving.

cúntəməlx ixíʔ łə‿x̌lap mi ʔal’uʔscútəlx x̌əl iʔ‿ksqəstnúm’cəlx.

The Animal People were excited and each hoped

iʔ‿tmixʷ tałt iʔ‿sk’ʷłáxsəlx uł yaʕt n’tílsəlx caʔkʷ cniłc

to get the most important name and the most important

iʔ‿kskʷənuʔis iʔ‿misx̌əc’x̌ác’t iʔ‿skʷist uł iʔ‿missílxʷaʔ

job.

tə‿sck’ul’.

Coyote was excited too. Most of the Animal People didn’t like

snk’lip talíʔ k’ʷłax nixʷ. k’ík’əm yaʕt iʔ‿tmixʷ lut t’ə‿x̌mínksəlx

Coyote.

snk’lip.

They said he bragged too much about himself

scútxəlx məł ałíʔ əcwuʔsn’cút xʷʔit k’əl i‿cucáwts

and pretended to know everything,

uł əck’ʷaʔk’ʷúlsts cniłc iʔ‿acmistís yaʕt stim’,

even when he did not know very much.

iwá lut qʷaʕy t’a‿cmistís iʔ‿stim’.

Coyote wanted to get a good name with an important job,

snk’lip x̌əmínks tə‿x̌ast tə‿skʷist uł tə‿x̌əc’x̌ác’t t‿sck’ʷul,

so everyone would look up to him and praise him a lot.

məł cmay yaʕt kəcsílxʷaʔstəm uł kəcwisiʔstəm niʕíp.

"I will be the first one at the name-giving," Coyote
"incá knkscxˀítaˀx iˀ‿k'əl‿sqəstnúm'," snk'lip xʷəxʷ
bragged to anyone who would listen.
wuˀsən'cút k'əl xiˀmíx swit iˀ‿ack'ək'níaˀmstəm.
"I think I would like to be Grizzly Bear and a Chief of the animals.
"kn‿ntils caˀkʷ kiláwna ikskʷíst uł kilmxʷíplaˀn iˀ‿ack'núsəs.
Maybe I would like to be Eagle and be a Chief of the
kəm' caˀkʷ kn‿məlqnúps uł kilmxʷíplaˀn yaˁt
flying creatures,
iˀ‿act'əxʷtíl'x,
or maybe Salmon and be a Chief of all the things that live
kəm' kn‿ntityíx məł kilmxʷíplaˀn yaˁt iˀ‿ack'əwwílx
in the water."
k'a‿nixʷtítkʷ."

Coyote's twin brother Fox happened to hear him.

snk'lip iʔ‿sncaʕpsíw'sc, x̌ʷaʕylxʷ əck'ək'níaʔmstəm.

Fox knew what Coyote was like and was ashamed of

x̌ʷaʕylxʷ əcmistís snk'lip iʔ‿ank'ʷúl'məns uɫ c'aʔxmís

his brother.

iʔ‿slax̌ts.

"Do not be too sure, Brother," he warned.

"lut miyáɫ akcmilsmíst iʔ‿l‿stim'," x̌aʔntím.

"Maybe no one will be allowed to choose their name.

"cmay lut swit t'‿ksnk'ʷaʔk'ʷíniʔs iʔ‿kskʷisc.

Maybe everyone will just have to take what is given.

cmay yaʕt swit kə‿ctxət'stís stim' iʔ‿sxʷíc'əc'xsəlx.

"That brother of mine always talks so smart," Coyote thought.

"ix̌waʔ ixíʔ isláx̌t niʕíp əcnpəx̌pəx̌cnscút," ntils snk'lip.

"I'll show him this time!" Coyote was always trying

"ikscaʔcúnmaʔm ʕapnáʔ!" snk'lip aɫíʔ niʕíp x̌minks

to prove he was smarter than Fox.

ksəck'ʷaʔnsxíxmiʔsc cniɫc iʔ‿mispəx̌páx̌t k‿təl‿x̌ʷaʕylxʷ.

So Coyote said to his brother, "You'll see.

tliʔ ki cus isláx̌ts, "n'ín'wis wikntxʷ.

You'll have to be nice to me when I am Chief."

anwí kʷu‿akəcx̌síkstmnəm kn‿ɫ‿il'mxʷílx.

"Oh, go to sleep, Coyote," his brother said, laughing,

"ix̌waʔ, xʷuyx pul'xəx, snk'lip" cut isláx̌ts uł kaʕyncútmntəm,

"or else you won't be up in time for the name-giving.

"ałíʔ cəm' lut aksxʷt'ílx mi ƛ'mipstxʷ iʔ‿skʷəsnúm'.

You always sleep in."

niʕíp kʷ‿əck'łʔatətxnúm't.

Coyote got angry. "Just for that," he thought, "I'm going to

snk'lip xʷəxʷ ʕaymt. "x̌əl itlíʔ," iʔ‿scəntílsc, "incá ikskswítm mi

stay awake all night,

kn‿kcqəłqíłtaʔx məł xƛ'ap iʔ‿sk'laxʷ,

just to make sure I get there first. I'm not going to sleep at all!"

kəcmí·ʔax kn‿kəcxʔítaʔx. lut kn‿t'‿ksʔítxaʔx!"

He was still feeling very angry as he went to his tipi

pútiʔ səcnq'əlsncútx ki xʷuy iʔ‿k'əl‿sxʷul'łxʷs

where his wife Mole was sitting by the door.

ilíʔ iʔ‿náx̌ʷnəx̌ʷs púl'laʔxʷ ki k'łnʔamtíp.

"Mole, gather lots of wood. I'm going to sit up all night,"

"Pul'axʷ, kamislp'x təxʷʔit. Kn‿ksmutax məł xƛ̓'pulaxʷ,"

Coyote said. Mole did as she was told.

snk'lip cut. Pul'axʷ ixiʔ k'ʷuls iʔ cułtm.

Coyote built a big fire to keep himself awake, and there he sat.

snk'lip tałáʔ iʔ‿sckp'nísəlp's x̌əl ksəcqəłqíłts, uł xiʔ mut ilíʔ.

Before the night was half over, however, Coyote's

iʔ‿lútiʔ iʔ‿snkʷəkʷʔác t'ə‿tx̌əyús, way' sic, snk'lip

eyes began to get heavier and heavier.

istk'ʷəƛ̕'k'ʷƛ̕'ústəns nəsnəstwˤálx.

He couldn't seem to keep them open!

xʷu··y uł lut t'a‿cqəłnústs łə‿kəctxʷəpxʷəpúsc.

Suddenly, he had an idea. He said, "I'll prop my eyes open,

kmíɬəm kiʔ k'əɬpaʔx̌x̌íʔst. ki cut, "n'i'n'wiʔs kən‿kt'əkt'ksəncút,

that way I won't fall asleep. Gosh, I'm so smart."

xiʔ məɬ lut iksʔatətxíʔst. way' uɬ kən‿pax̌páx̌t."

So he broke some little twigs and propped his eyes open.

xiʔ ckəm'ám sx̌ʷəƛ"íkstn uɬ kt'ət'əksəncút.

Then he sat back. "Hah!" he thought, "Now I'll be there first."

xiʔ skɬaʔqínmiʔsts. xi··ntils "ixíʔ mi cxʔit kən‿kicx."

However, the Great Spirit had plans for Coyote,

náx̌əmɬ, iʔ‿k'ʷəl'əncútn way' ksck'əɬk'ʷúl' x̌əl sənk'líp,

so he caused Coyote to go to sleep anyway,

ki k'ʷul's sənk'líp ɬə‿ksʔítxs iwá,

with his eyes wide open.

t'i kiryírs.

Soon it was morning and time for all the Animal People

xʷuy uł way' x̌əlpúlaʔxʷ uł k'łkicx iʔ‿sc'áx̌səlx iʔ‿tmixʷ

to receive their names.

łə‿ksxʷíc'əc'xsəlx tə‿kskʷístsəlx.

Coyote slept and slept. The Animal People kept going by

snk'lip əc'i··tx niʕíp. i‿tmixʷ yaʕt txʷúwilxsəlx

and looking at him.

uł yaʕt ʕác'səlx.

"What's wrong with Coyote's eyes?", they asked each other,

"sta· mat səc'kínx snk'lip iʔ‿stk'ʷəƛ̓'k'ʷƛ̓'ústns?" sunwíxʷəlx,

laughing.

uł ʕayʕayncútəlx.

"He just sits there with his eyes wide open."

"mu··t náx̌əmł t'i kir'yír's"

Mole knew he was asleep but she wouldn't wake him.

púl'laʔxʷ əcmistís səc'ítxəx náx̌əmł lut t'ə‿qiłs.

She did not want him to become a great Chief,

ałíʔ cniłc lut t'ə x̌əmínks łə‿ksil'ləmxʷíl'xs tə‿sílxʷaʔ,

because she loved him just the way he was.

ałíʔ p'uƛ̓m x̌minks t'i kmix cniłc iʔ‿ank'ʷúlməns.

Finally, Coyote woke up. He ran to the gathering place
taʔkən'uxʷ, snk'lip ki qiłt. xʷət'pncút k'əl‿ksnʔúl'uʔstnsəlx
as fast as he could.
t'iʔ tə‿xʷus.
No one was there but the Great Spirit Chief.
Lut swit t'ə‿ilíʔ t'i‿kmax iʔ‿k'ʷəl'ncútn.
Coyote thought he was the first one there.
snk'lip ntils cniłc iʔ‿acxʔit iʔ‿kicx ilíʔ.

"I want to be named Chief of all the animals!" he shouted
"inx̌mínk kn‿kłilmíxʷm x̌əl yaʕt iʔ‿tmixʷ!" st'əqʷcíns
happily.
t'i‿npi·ls.
The Great Spirit slowly shook his head.
iʔ‿k'ʷəl'ncútn tə‿k'ək'aʔlí pəkʷqínxtm.

"You are too late," he said. "Grizzly Bear left early this morning."
"way' kʷ‿ƛ'mip," cuntm. "kiláwna way' nis t‿siłkʷəkʷáʕst"

"Well then," answered Coyote, "let me be Chief of all
"kʷaʔ nák'ʷəm," cut snk'lip, "kn‿kłilmíxʷm x̌əl yaʕt
the flying things.
a‿ct'əxʷtíl'x.
Give me the name of Eagle." Again, the Great Spirit
caʔkʷ kʷu‿xʷic'łtxʷ ikskʷíst məlqnúps." itíʔ iʔ‿k'ʷəl'ncútn
shook his head.
əłpəkʷntís iʔ‿c'aʔsíqəns.

"No Coyote, all the names have been given out, except for one.

“lut snk’lip, yaʕyáʕt iʔ‿skʷist way’ xʷic’xmn, t’i kmíx naqs.

All the jobs have been handed out.

yaʕt iʔ‿ksck’łtar’ waiʔ kc’x̌ʷəx̌ʷíplaʔn.

All the plants, animals, birds, insects and

iʔ‿spəl’úlaʔxʷ, a‿ck’núsəs, a‿ct’əxʷtílx a‿c’akʷtíl’x uł

things that live in the water have gone to their

iʔ‿acxʷəlxʷált k’a‿nixʷtítkʷ way’ xʷúyəlx k’əl‿mnímłcəlx

special places to live and do their jobs.

iʔ‿kłnxʷəlxʷəltánsəlx ksk’łtr’antisəlx.

Only your name is left, Coyote.

kmax askʷíst iʔ‿łəwísəlx, snk’lip.

No one wanted to steal it from you."

lut swit t’ə‿x̌əmínks łə‿kskʷiłts.”

At this, Coyote was very unhappy.

xiʔ uł snk’lip tałt iʔ‿sq’əlspuʔúsc.

He sank down on his knees and hung his head.

way’ uł q’ʷəyq’ʷəyxi·n’ uł kməx̌əx̌qín.

"Poor Coyote," thought the Great Spirit. "I cannot let him

“ámsəm, snk’lip,” ntils iʔ‿k’ʷəl’ncútn. “lut t’iksxiʔxiʔstím

feel so bad."

myəł łə‿ksq’əlspuʔúsc.”

"Get up, Coyote," he said. "I made you sleep late

"tíłxəx, snk'lip," cúntəm. "incá ispuʔús ki kʷ‿k'łʔatətxənúmt

because I have a special job for you.

ałí kn‿ksck'ʷúl' kmax k'‿anwí.

I sent you to the land of dreams on purpose.

kʷulstmn iʔ‿k'əl‿sqíʔslaʔxʷ t'iʔ t‿ispuʔús.

I have lots of work for you to do before the People-To-Be

k‿ałí xʷʔit inx̌mínk aksck'ʷúl mi sic ciyáˁp iʔ‿st'əlsqílxʷ

come to live here."

łə‿ksəcxʷəl'xʷáltcəlx aláʔ."

"Really!" Coyote asked, jumping up happily to his feet.

"ha uníxʷ!" snk'lip cut, t'iʔ car'i·k tə‿snpiyílsc əłc'əlál.

The Great Spirit nodded and said,

iʔ‿k'ʷəl'ncútn q'ʷət'sám uł cuntm,

"In this world there are a lot of things that will be

"axáʔ aláʔ iʔ‿l‿tmxʷúlaʔxʷ cəm' kłnxʷaʔmíw's iʔ‿stim'

harmful to the People-To-Be.

iʔ‿kłnx̌aʔnúmtns iʔ‿st'əlsqílxʷ.

The monsters that live here will destroy the

iʔ‿nʔałnaʔsqílxʷtn iʔ‿ʔaláʔlx ʕapnáʔ cəm' nc'əspúl'axʷsts

People-To-Be.

iʔ‿st'əlsqílxʷ.

There will be many hardships for them."

cəm' nxʷaʔmíw's i‿kłtkakʔústnsəlx."

"I will give you, Coyote, a special power to destroy these

"kʷ‿iksxʷíc'xtm, snk'lip, akłksisiyústn mi əckswílqstxʷ

monsters.

iʔ‿nʔałnaʔsqílxʷtn.

With your special power you will be able to change your shape

t‿asq'ʷastínk məł aksəcqəłnúnəm ł‿aksk'łʔaysncút

into anything you wish.

xiʔmíx iʔ‿tə‿stim' anx̌mínk.

You will be able to imagine things and make them happen.

n'us k'łpaʔsntíxʷ iʔ‿stim' məł ilíʔ əct'iʔc'xíł.

This power is given to you to use wisely.

ixíʔ iʔ‿sq'ʷaʔstínk akckʷúl'mnəm tə‿x̌ast.

It is given to you to help the People-To-Be."

asxʷíc'əc'x x̌əl iʔ‿kłnx̌əstáns iʔ‿st'əlsqílxʷ."

Coyote had thought he was happy before, but when he heard

snk'lip ntils talíʔ way' səcnpiyílsx, náx̌əmł łə‿níxəlms

these words,

iʔ‿tə‿qʷəlqʷílstm,

he was so excited that he ran around in circles, chasing his tail

ksxan iʔ‿scnpiyílsc uł xəlxalkmncút, ksnkcníkiʔs iʔ‿syupsc

and yapping for joy.

uł cəpcaʕpəpíʔst.

The Great Spirit shook his head and hid a smile as he watched

iʔ‿k'ʷəl'ncútn t'i pəkʷqínm uł wikʷs iʔ‿scnaʕyúsc ła‿c'ʕac'sts

Coyote frolic.

snk'lip ła‿cłət'łət'pílx.

"It is because of your foolish ways, however, that you will not

"ałí məł kʷ‿səcpsˤáyaʔx, məł cəm' lut yaˤyáˤt spən'kín mi

always be careful," he warned Coyote.

kʷ‿əctxet'míst," x̌aʔntís snk'lip.

"You may be killed, therefore, your twin brother Fox,

"łə‿pn'kin cmay kʷ‿ƛ'lal, x̌əl itlíʔ asncaʔpsíw's x̌ʷaˤylxʷ,

will accompany you and be near you always."

kskxəntsís uł niˤíp kstk'ik'tmnts."

"Fox will be given the special power to bring you back to life

"x̌ʷaˤylx̌ʷ ksxʷíc'əc'aʔx t‿kłksisiyústns ła‿cxʷəl'stúms

when you are killed.

ła‿claʔkín kʷ‿łaʔ‿cƛ'lal.

Even if all your bones are scattered all over,

iwá yaˤyáˤt asc'ím łaʔ‿cpəx̌ʷám yaˤt k'aʔkín,

if one hair remains,

uł iwá k'im t'i na·nqs tl‿anqəpqíntn,

Fox can step over it and bring you back to life.

x̌ʷaˤylxʷ kstk'ʷítxəlmiʔs məł kʷ‿łxʷəlál.

Go now and try to behave and do good. You are an important

xʷuyx ˤapnáʔ məł kswitntxʷ ł‿aksx̌əsmncút. anwí kʷ‿x̌aʔx̌áʔ

person now,"

tə‿sqilxʷ ˤapnáʔ,"

the Great Spirit said, sending Coyote away.

iʔ‿k'ʷəl'ncútn cuntm, uł kʷulsts itlíʔ.

The Great Spirit watched Coyote go. He knew

iʔ‿k’ʷəl’ncútn əc’ʕác’əsts snk’lip ki xʷuy. cmistís

how Coyote was.

iʔ‿cawts snk’lip.

He knew that Coyote would not do a perfect job.

cmistís snk’lip lut yaʕt isck’ʷul’s t’‿ksqʷámqʷəmtaʔx.

He knew Coyote would make mistakes, and there would still be

cmistís snk’lip ksəcxík’ək’aʔx, uł cəm’ pútiʔ xʷʔit

some hardships and sorrows for the People-To-Be.

iʔ‿kłtkaʔkʔústns uł iʔ‿kłkpaʔpaʔsílxtns iʔ‿st’əlsqílxʷ.

However, it was very important that everything on

náx̌amł, talí x̌əc’x̌ác’t tə‿sck’ʷul’ yaʕt stim’ aláʔ

this earth be given a purpose.

iʔ‿l‿tmxʷúlaʔxʷ kłkscəntər’ús.

Kou-Skelowh/We Are the People

An Okanagan Legend

HOW TURTLE SET THE ANIMALS FREE

xkiʔsts ʔarsíkʷ iʔ‿tmixʷ kiʔ łuníkəkst

Eagle was very fast. He raced all the Animal People

məlqnúps talíˀ ƛax̌t. q'ʷəq'ʷúƛ'aˀxsts yaʕt iˀ‿tmixʷ

and beat them.

uł ƛ'xʷúpntməlx.

Even Fox and Wolf lost. All the Animal People who lost

nixʷ x̌ʷaʕylxʷ naˀł nc'iˀcn ʕalápəlx. yaʕt iˀ‿tmixʷ ła‿cʕaláp

these races became Eagle's slaves.

iˀ‿l‿sq'ʷq'ʷƛ'áxn məł k'ʷúl'əl'x ta‿nk'ʷsaltktns məlqnúps.

Eagle was Chief of all the animals, except for Turtle

məlqnúps iʔ‿ilmíxʷm x̌əl yaʕt iʔ‿tmixʷ, kmax ʔar'síkʷ

who lived with his partner Muskrat.

ałi'ʔ smutx k'əl slax̌ts sʕ'aʔníxʷ.

They were free because they were the only ones who did not

pútiʔ əck'ʷíxʷəlx ałíʔ mnímłcəlx t'iʔ ckmáxəlx iʔ‿lut

race Eagle.

t'ə q'ʷəq'ʷúƛ'aʔxənmstsəlx məlqnúps.

They knew they could not run very fast, but one night

əcmistísəlx lut talíʔ t'ə ƛ'áx̌təlx, náx̌əmł naqs sk'laxʷ

Turtle had a dream.

ʔar'sík'ʷ qiʔs.

He was told, "You must race

cuntm t‿smipnúm'ts, "anwí aksənk'ʷłq'ʷəq'ʷúƛ'aʔxnəm

Eagle tomorrow to free the Animal People.

məlqnúps mi łunikəkstms iʔ‿tmixʷ.

They must be free when the People-To-Be come."

yaʕyáʕt kəcłunikstax mi ciyʕáp iʔ‿st'əlsqílxʷ."

In the morning, Turtle told Muskrat, "Get up!

łə‿x̌əlpúl'aʔxʷ, ʔar'síkʷ cus sʕ'aʔníxʷ, "xʷət'ílxəx!

Go for a swim!

xʷuyx cʕál'xəx!

Get ready! We must race Eagle."

x̌əcmncútx! ksq'ʷəq'ʷúƛ'aʔxstəm məlqnúps."

"You cannot beat him, Turtle!" Muskrat said unhappily,

"lut t'‿aksƛ'xʷúpm, ʔar'síkʷ!" sʕ'aʔníxʷ cut t'i nlútəls,

"You cannot beat him! He flies too fast."

"lut t'‿aksƛ'xʷúpm! ła‿ct'uxʷt miyáł ƛ'ʕax̌t".

"I know. All of our people lost before, but my dream told me
“əcmistín. yaʕt isnəqsílxʷtət ʕaláp way’, náx̌əmɬ isqíʔs kʷu‿cus
to race and win," Turtle replied.
q’ʷəq’ʷúƛ’xənx məɬ kʷ‿ƛ’xʷup,” cut ʔar’síkʷ

Together the two friends went to Eagle's camp.
iʔ‿ɬax̌tíw’s xʷúy’ilx k’əl snilíʔtns məlqnúps.
Turtle told Eagle, "I want to race with you
ʔar’síkʷ cus məlqnúps, “inx̌mínk kʷ‿iksq’ʷəq’ʷuƛ’aʔxstm
tomorrow."
ɬə‿x̌lap”

"All right, Turtle," Eagle answered. "Tomorrow we race,

“way’, ʔar’síkʷ,” cut məlqnúps. “x̌lap mi kʷu‿q’ʷəq’ʷƛ’áxnəm,

when the sun comes up.

put łck’ʷƛap iʔ‿x̌yałnxʷ.

If you win, the Animal People are yours."

kʷ‿ł‿ƛ’xʷup, yaʕt iʔ‿tmixʷ anwí kc’x̌ʷíplaʔntxʷ.”

"Yes," Turtle agreed.

“huhúy,” way’ xʔínaʔ ʔar’síkʷ.

"If I win, Turtle, I will keep you here.

“incá kn‿ł‿ƛ’xʷup, ʔar’síkʷ, kʷ‿iksc’x̌ʷipláʔm aláʔ.

You are betting your life on this race."

ascx̌ác ascxʷəlxʷált axáʔ iʔ‿l‿sq’ʷəq’ʷúƛ’aʔxən.”

As Turtle crawled away, all the Animal People laughed,

xiˀ itlíˀ ˀar'síkʷ sˀukʷts, yaˁt iˀ‿tmixʷ ˁayˁayncútsəlx,

because they did not think they would ever be free.

ałíˀ lut t'a ntílsəlx pənkín t'‿ksłunikəkstáxəlx.

Next day, Turtle met Eagle for the race. Eagle told him,

x̌əlpúlaʔxʷ, ʔar’sikʷ tkic məlqnúps. məlqnúps cuntm,

"Choose your place, Turtle.

"nk’ʷaʔk’ʷínx t‿akłnq’ʷəq’ʷƛ’áxtn, ʔar’síkʷ.

I will race you any distance you decide."

kʷ‿iksq’ʷəq’ʷúƛ’aʔxstm xiʔmíx ksl’kuts akscnk’ʷaʔk’ʷín."

"Any place?" Turtle asked.

"xiʔmíx laʔkín?" siwntm tə‿ʔar’síkʷ.

Eagle replied, "Our people hear me.

məlqnúps cut, "p‿isnəqsílxʷ kʷu‿níxlməntp.

Any place, Turtle."

x̌iʔmíx laʔkín, ʔar’síkʷ."

Quickly Turtle said, "Then carry me up in the air,

tə‿xʷus cuntm tə‿ʔar’síkʷ, " huhúy kʷaʔ kʷu‿nwísəlxnt,

Eagle. I will tell you when to drop me.

məlqnúps. łə‿cúntsən mi kʷu‿łuníkstməntxʷ.

From there we will race.

itlíʔ mi kʷu‿q’ʷəq’ʷúƛ’aʔxnəm.

Whoever reaches the ground first

swit ksk’łkíciʔs iʔ‿təmxʷúlaʔxʷ iʔ‿kə‿cxʔítaʔx

wins the race."

iʔ‿ksƛ’xʷúpaʔx."

Eagle began to get worried. He took Turtle high up.

məlqnúps xiʔ sk'łpaʔsncúts. nwísəlxts ʔar'síkʷ k'a‿nwist.

When Turtle yelled, "Let go!"

xʷu··y ʔar'sík'ʷ t'əqʷcín, "kʷu‿łuníkstmnt!"

Eagle dropped him.

məlqnúps xiʔ łuníkstmntm.

He fell like a rock. Eagle tried to catch up to him.

yaxʷt c'x̌ił tə‿xƛ'ut. məlqnúps kswits łə ksnkəcníkns.

Turtle stuck out his head.

ʔar'síkʷ ƛ'iksms iʔ‿c'áʔsyqəns.

"E-e-eee! Hurry, Eagle! I will beat you!"

"i-i-iiiiii! xʷustx, məlqnúps! cəm' ƛ'əxʷúpntsən!"

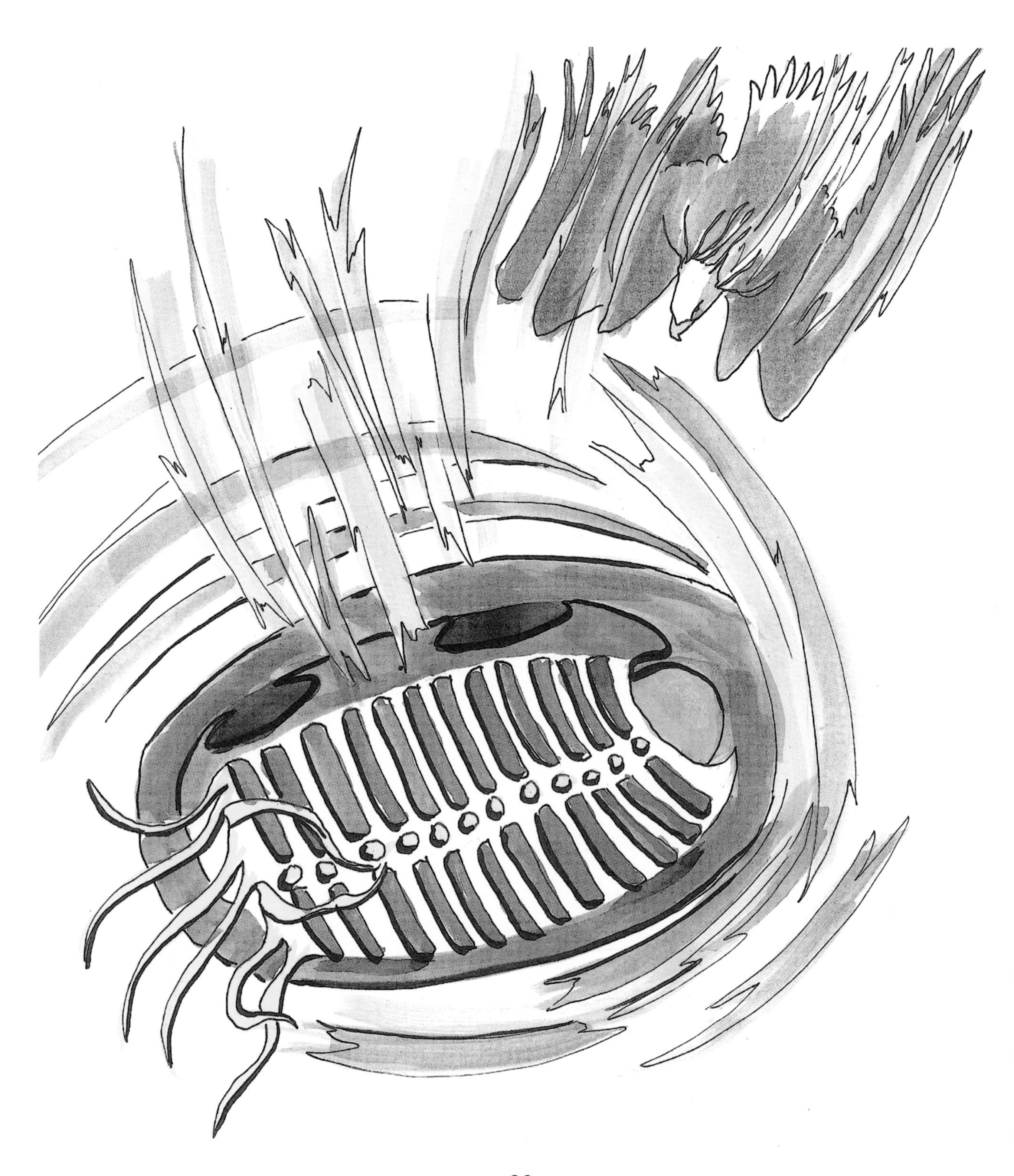

Then Turtle pulled his head in and fell faster.

xiʔ ł‿ncəkʷntís iʔ‿c'áʔsyqəns uł itlíʔ misƛ'áx̌t i‿scyaxʷts.

The Animal People watched. They all shouted for Turtle.

yaʕt iʔ‿tmixʷ əcyaʔyáx̌aʔ. yaʕt xʷʕaʔntísəlx ʔar'síkʷ.

Muskrat jumped around and his tail whipped the air.

sʕ'aʔníxʷ łət'łat'pmncút uł iʔ‿syupsc t'iʔ łəʔc'úp, łəʔc'úp.

His partner was winning. Eagle was close!

iʔ‿slax̌ts way' səcƛ'xʷúpx. məlqnúps nk'ək'ní·kn!

He thought, "Turtle will hit the ground like a rock!"

ntils, "ʔar'síkʷ cəm' nc'əq'əq'úlaʔxʷ c'x̌ił tə‿xƛ'ut!"

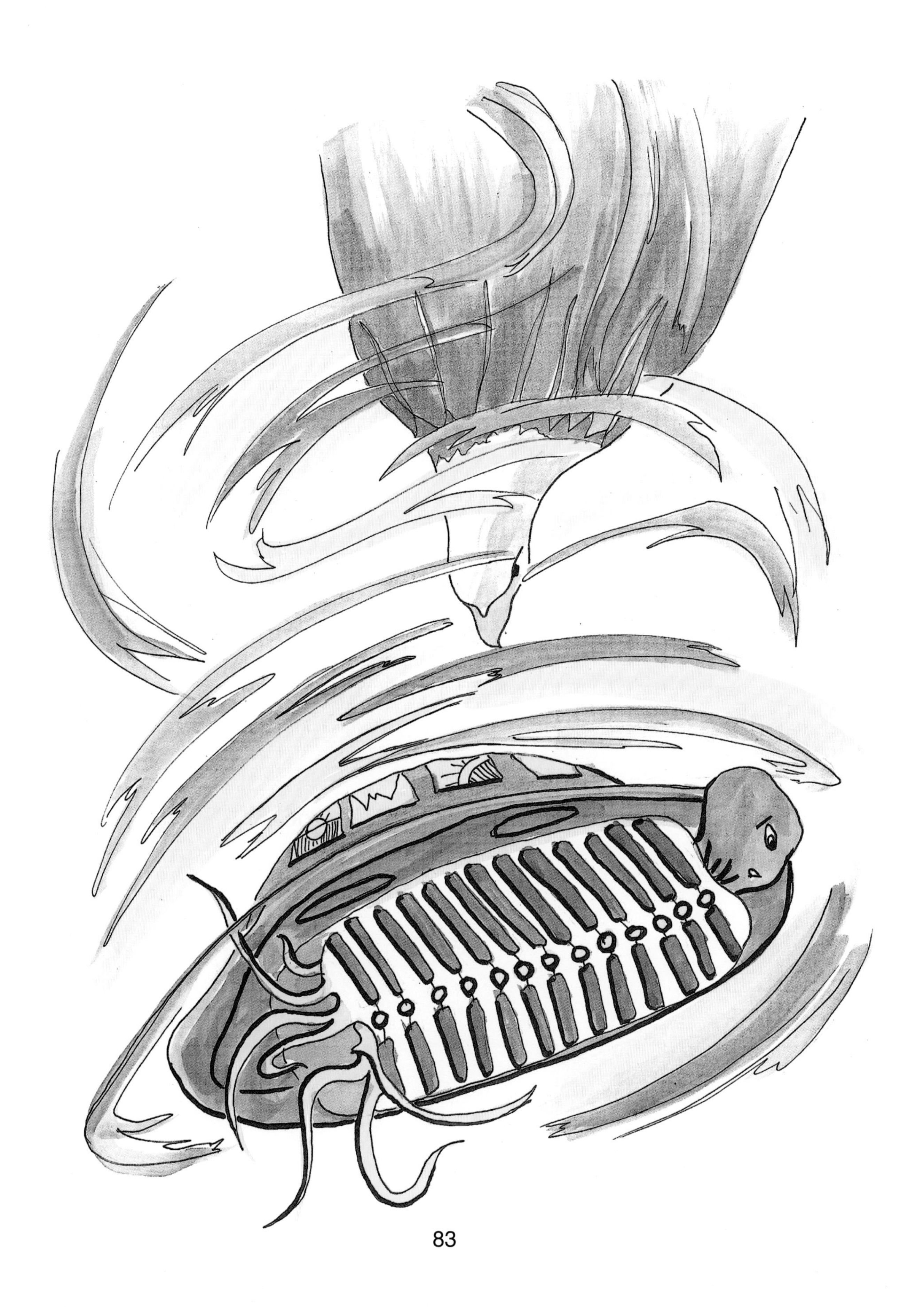

Turtle did, but he stood up and told the Animal People,

ʔar’síkʷ tiʔx̌ílm, náx̌əmɬ tiɬx uɬ cus iʔ‿tmixʷ,

"Now I will be Chief in making this decision.

"ʕapnáʔ incá kn‿kɬilmíxʷm iʔ‿l‿ksck’ɬtar’tət.

You are free. Go where you like,

p‿yaʕyáʕt p‿k’ʷíxʷəxʷ. xʷúywi, k’ákin kɬx̌mínkmp,

Animal People. Anywhere!"

iʔ‿p‿tmixʷ. xiʔmíx laʔkín!"

The Animal People scattered. They would tell the People-To-Be

xiʔ iʔ‿tmixʷ spəx̌ʷməncúts. ix̌iʔ ksmayɬtí··s iʔ‿st’əlsqílxʷ

about the first races.

iʔ‿acxʔít iʔ‿sq’ʷəq’ʷúƛ’aʔxn.

Turtle spoke to Eagle, "You know,

ʔar'síkʷ qʷəlqʷílsts məlqnúps, "əcmistíxʷ,

I cannot always beat you, Eagle,

lut pnkin kʷ‿t'‿iksƛ'xʷúpm, məlqnúps,

but I had a dream, and I learned how to beat you.

náx̌əmł kn‿qiʔs, uł mipnún kʷ‿ł‿iksƛ'xʷúpm.

I will never overtake your speed.

lut pnkin kʷ‿t'‿iksmisƛ'áx̌t tl‿anwí.

You will always be the fastest one.

anwí niʕíp kʷ‿ksmisƛ'áx̌taʔx.

You will always catch what you want to eat.

niʕíp akəckʷnúnm aksc'íłn.

When the People-To-Be come, they will dream too,

iʔ‿st'əlsqílxʷ łcyʕap, mnímłcəlx kəcqíʔsaʔx nixʷ,

and they will learn from their dreams.

uł kəcmipnwíłnaʔx iʔ‿tl‿sqíʔscəlx.

Just as I did."

c'x̌ił t‿incá."